WARNING: This book contains graphic content surrounding sensitive topics that readers may find triggering, including suicide, sexual violence, and other numerous forms of abuse and violence. Reader discretion is advised.

If you or anyone you know needs help finding support or crisis resources, please go to SuicidePreventionLifeline.org.

For Christina, and all of the smiles that faded.

PAST, PRESENT,

ALTERNATIVE:

NIGHTFALL

LEILANI

GRACEFFA

First paperback edition December 2018

Book cover design by Leilani Graceffa

ISBN 978-1-7335558-1-4
ISBN 978-1-7335558-0-7 (hardcover)
ISBN 978-1-7335558-2-1 (ebook)

For more information, visit www.leilanigraceffa.com.

I

"I EXPECTED YOU TO BE a little bit taller. You're an adorable little woman." The corners of his mouth curve upwards as he tries to put a lulling smile on his face at me.

"Ian," Mom furrows her eyebrows, "she doesn't like being made fun of for her height. Just because you're the tallest person in this house…"

My plump legs hover at least two feet over the hardwood floor with me sitting in this wooden barstool. "I'm used to it, mom." I chuckle. "Thank you for the compliment though."

My brother nods his head before shifting his body back into his chair, then turns his head towards mom and asks, "Why are you still down here? It's almost your bedtime."

With her hairstreak grey eyes, she shoots a rather angry glare towards her son as if he had given her an offence. "You could've just said you would like to be alone with your sis—"

"Mom," He seizes her, "go to bed, please."

"Fine." She frowns. "Goodnight, kids."

"Goodnight, mom." It's hard to believe she still holds onto the habit of calling us kids even though we are now adults fresh out of college.

As soon as my brother strides up the steps shooing our mother up the stairs, my phone lets out a pulse. I extend my arm out behind me to grasp my phone from the back pocket of my jeans. A text from my boyfriend,

2

Shane, who is back in Toronto, Ontario finishing his last semester in college.

Ian comes pacing back into the kitchen while I have my nose buried in my phone screen, mutters a personal comment like, "I hate... [something]" to himself before settling back into his chair. And the first question he asks me is, "Who's your bae?"

I raise my head, "Why?"

"Because," He smiles slyly, "I'm nosy, and I want to know about the guy or girl that asked you out. You never told me you're already in a relationship."

Okay... "His name is Shane, and I met him during my second year of studies."

He grumbles. "What's his surname?"

"Garrett."

"You're dating that asshole? Ponytail Shane, with the eyebrow piercing? I'm surprised he even found you attractive."

"He's not an asshole." I frown. "Y'all know each other?"

He slowly nods his head. "That's what he wants you to believe."

He was disconsolate when I first met him. He still never told me the reason he was so upset, and why he has so many blocked numbers on his phone. "Then you might know the reason he was so upset before."

"Who we're talking about?"

"Never mind…"

"I'm kidding," He snickers. "I don't know why he was upset."

"I can tell." I lower my eyes from him, "I expected dad to be here. I haven't seen him since God knows when."

"Neither have I."

"We don't have the same father."

Ian sighs, "I know. I haven't seen my dad in a thousand years either. I've been asking and asking, mom still won't answer the question."

"Do you think she's hiding it?"

"What is one thing she doesn't hide?"

"That she might've butchered her own parents to death."

"Teddie…" He laughs, "Teddie told you that story, didn't she?"

"No, my dad did, and I used to believe it." Why did she feel the need to lie to us? I don't think she's ever considered telling us about each other—or even wanted to inform us about each other—until two years ago. But I bet our dads would've eventually said something if they knew about each other; she lied to them too. And she continues to lie.

He begins to watch my fingers hastily tap onto letters on the keyboard on my phone screen so keenly that I am almost able to feel his eyes burning into the skin of my hands. "You're so honest about being nosy." He stays quiet with his lips pressed into a firm line. "IAN, NO!" I exclaim at him when he abruptly swipes my phone from my hands. "GIVE ME…"

"You girls are so obsessed with your phones."

To keep me from retrieving my device from him, he wields one of my weaknesses; challenging my height, by hoisting my phone into the air with his other hand while I make a hassle attempting to reach across him with my short arms. "I'm not obsessed with it. I keep important information on it. You've never had one?"

"I do have one," He assures, "but I have better things to do than be on a device all day."

"That's good, for you. Can I have my phone back, please?"

Instead of politely handing me back the device, he lets his right hand descend from mid-air before plastering a bright, wicked smile on his face with his lips that forces me to spout a cackle from my stomach. "Why are you smiling like that?" I ask.

He parts his lips, "You want your phone back?"

"Yes, please…"

"Kiss me."

"Excuse me?"

"You heard me."

"Are you kidding me?" Why would he want me to kiss him? "Why? Do I have to?"

His smile alters into a smug one, "Unless you still want to reach for it."

I purse my lips together. Ian would make me look like a little six-year-old trying to reach for her favourite Barbie. He's probably not going to let loose until I give in to giving him a smooch. "Fine." I roll my eyes. I shift my body forward in my chair, contract my lips, then lightly press my nose against his right cheek.

He grins, this time with his cheekbones flaunting themselves. "You're a good kisser."

"Thanks… I guess."

"Here's your precious phone back, ma'am."

———

My brother sits with his legs crossed on the couch cushion beside me in nothing other than plaid pyjama bottoms that are as vapid blue as beneath a shelf cloud just before a severe thunderstorm.

Inflamed grazes as faintly rouge as red paint etching off of the soddened bristles of a watercolour paintbrush corrode into the skin of his back as if he invaded the well-cherished territory of a miffed house cat. "What happened to yo—"

"My back," He quickly catches the remaining of my question. "Something is in here with us, and it's not human."

"Is it an animal?"

"It's a demon, and it won't leave me alone." He replies with the rather unsettling answer passively. The calm cadence of his voice while telling me the answer causes the baby hairs on my nape to sprout. I immediately furrow my brows, "And you're okay with it attacking you?"

"No, I can't do much about it, that's why I'm constantly burning smudge sticks while mom is asleep."

"Why while she's asleep?"

"She hates the smell of it."

Maybe she is the demon, but I doubt she'd hurt Ian like one.

"You remind me of a character from a book series." Says Ian while his nose is buried in the scriptures and hymns of the Holy Bible.

"Who?" I turn my head to catch an amusing smirk slowly creeping upon his face. "If you say what I think you're about to say, I will smack you upside the head with that Bible. I have nothing in common with her."

"What was I about to say?"

"A— —."

"Hell no," He chuckles, "it's L— —."

"Why?"

"Because your hair is dyed platinum blonde like hers. I used to have a huge crush on her. Why'd you think of — — — —?"

"Because Shane still says I look like her." One of the reasons I decided to dye my hair blonde in the first place because I was annoyed that even my friends were starting to agree with him about it.

"You don't look anything like her."

"I know," I lower my head, proceeding to scroll through pins of bunnies on Pinterest. I used to own a rabbit named Calypso; she lived a good nine years before I came home to find her dead after coming back from school one afternoon.

"You need to stay away from that phone." Ian insists, shortly after setting his Bible down, then pecking me on the cheek.

Says every parent nowadays. I snicker, "Make me."

"I insist."

When he snatches the device from my hands and hurls it over the coffee table onto the chair adjacent to the couch, I gain the requested nerve to yell at him, "Ian, what the hell! I didn't mean literally!"

"You asked for it." He extends both of his arms out to hustle me back down onto the couch. I begin to writhe my body between the pillows and throw my hands at him when he doesn't hesitate for even a second attempting to tear away at my clothing. "What are you doing?! IAN!"

As if I purposely triggered him by pushing an aggressive button in his brain, he cinches my right arm down onto the cushion with one of his hands and takes a firm grasp on the fringe of my track pants with his other. Then he snarls at me, "Stop fighting me." Gripping my bottoms by the waistline, he lowers them from my waist until they surround my ankles.

"Stop!" I continue attempting to throw and swat at him with my left hand until he catches my lower jaw in a firm clutch, then constrains my head to force our faces to meet. "Leave me alone!"

"Stop squirming." The sorely passive tone in his voice once again sends the hairs on my nape sprouting. This isn't okay.

But he proceeds to intrude me with himself; after I plead for him to stop. And he finishes inside of me with sheer indulgence on his face and the potential of virtue in his eyes.

2

"RAELYNN?" I HEAR MOM UTTER my name indistinctly as she rests a hand on my back and gently shakes me into consciousness.

Instead of ignoring her and dozing off, I try my best to make out an answer to her through the distress and grogginess, "Yea…?"

"Your food is getting cold. Come downstairs and eat it."

"Mhmm…" Everything aches. I doubt mom would believe the real reason Ian shooed her away so early last night.

With the metal fork mom handed me in my left hand, I idly prong at the hot scrambled eggs on the platter in front of me, while mom stares fixedly at me not scarfing down the food (like I usually would be) from across the table.

"You're not going to eat, are you?"

I let the silverware fall from my hand onto the plate, "I'm not hungry."

"Something happened last nig—"

"Nothing happened." I scowl. "Where's Ian?"

"I haven't seen him all morning."

I quickly stand up from my chair. "I'll be back."
Even though I feel like lying on the floor in a fetal posi-

tion to bawl my eyeballs out of their sockets, I'm not going to make what he did to me last night seem okay, or let him presume that I'm okay with it. "IAN!"

My screech causes my brother to jolt up from the chair he's sitting in. "Jesus, Raelynn!" He furrows his brows, "Screaming at this time of the day?"

"You know why, you fucking asshole! You raped me!"

He hesitates rather quickly, head turned and gazing widely at me with his luna green eyes through the lens of his glasses as if I had just spoken to him in a bizarre language before attempting to alter the subject with, "Did you take that morning after pill I gave you?"

"What the fuck? Don't change the subject!"

"Okay," He sighs, "I'm sorry, Raelynn. I've realized what I did, and I feel like a sack of shit. I'm sorry." The usual bland tone of his voice indicates he is only half-assing his apology.

I lower my eyes. "You don't mean it."

"Raelynn…"

———

I don't understand. Of course, I don't understand. What goes through the heads of people before they carry out a life-altering action? For instance: murder and rape. When you look into the pupils of a lot of these people's eyes, you see absolutely nothing, but abyssal blackness. It's different when you look into the pupils of an individual with a soul.

Light illuminates the eyes of individuals with one and ingresses the eyes of individuals without one.

Most people are born with one, and the corruption of this world eventually causes the demons and maybe even the devil himself to plague them. Then they inflict their own demons onto others. It's almost like the Black Plague; except that got around faster.

"Why are you out here by yourself?" Mom asks.

"Why not?" I frown. "I'm watching the snow fall. I have nothing else to do, yet."

"Alright little puffin," She says before striding towards my hammock, "what's going on?"

"Nothing's going on."

"You slept later than usual, and you didn't eat this morning, and you screamed at your brother, so obviously something is wrong. And where is your phone?"

"Did you just call me a little puffin? Okay, now I know you've been around my dad lately, and you just aren't telling me anything. I have no idea where my phone is, and I don't care about it right now."

She slowly nods her head. "When are you coming back in?"

"Probably never, why?"

She parts her lips, and before she gets to answer my question, one of the doors from the inside of my bedroom sways open behind mom. "Mom?" We hear Ian utter from behind the door. "Yes, Ian?"

"Teddie is downstairs waiting for you."

The woman rolls her eyes, then replies with an annoyed, "I'm coming."

For some reason even after having Ian and me, she still hasn't repaired the burnt bridge for her younger sister, Theodora (Teddie). They are still raging rivals from childhood, and they don't possess the typical sibling rivalry. According to the scarring stories Teddie tells me about their extant competition, mom has always been the combatant, and she has always been the arbitrator of their relationship.

"Will you answer my question, please, little sister?"

"What's the question?"

"Did you take that pill I left on your nightstand?"

"Maybe."

My brother utters a sigh before lowering his head in guilt. "I know you're still pissed off at me, Raelynn..."

"Oh, it's not about last night anymore." I quickly assure. "Your apology to me this morning was half-assed, and I don't appreciate it. Now you expect me to get it over it?"

"You heard me wrong."

"I heard you wrong?" I snarl before turning my head away from the screening separating the balcony from outside. "I listened to your voice, and you didn't mean it. You are officially a sack of shit. Go exorcize your demon, it needs you to provoke it."

"Brutal," He says in the same voice blatantly.

"Leave me alone, please." He grows impatient enough to refuse to pursue my desire to be alone. Refusing to leave me to myself, he gets only a couple of steps away from the door before I prohibit him from getting any closer to me by snapping, "STOP!"

"Raelynn," He furrows his brows at me, "I don't want to hurt you."

"You wish I could believe that. Go away."

"I'm sorry."

"Sure you are." Without a second request, he turns his back to me, then leaves.

What is so difficult about giving a hearted apology? Nobody looks into each other's eyes to provide willing apologies anymore.

———

"I brought you into this world, and I can take you out." A voice, similar to mom's indistinctly echoes.

I grab a pair of my runners set aside my bed, but I don't even bother to put them on before going downstairs and stepping out onto the damp, icy wood of the platform deck. The hypnotic voice intoning the lyrics to a song begins to grow emphatic in my ears as I'm twisting and turning in the seam of my darkening surroundings and the sun proceeds to conceal itself before a mass of forest.

Adjacent to the house, across the vast, icebound lake converging the acres, a dim light steadily illuminates inside of something the shape of a vertical rectangle— like a lantern.

The singing doesn't stop. It starts to rip echoes into the silent air as I roam across the thick ice towards the dim light. "Ian?"

He doesn't answer me; keeping his back facing me while spading snow-covered soil aside a steep hollow in the earth. And laying cold and inert in the pit of dirt is our mother's body. With a wry look in his eyes, he shoots a glower towards me and lets the shovel fall from his hands before grabbing a matchstick and streaking the head of it against an igniter, and then tossing the lit stick into the pit.

———

My left arm is extended up above me when I jerk awake, still on the balcony in my hammock. "Jesus…" I don't hesitate to roll myself out of the quilt onto the floor. "Mom!" Nobody replies. "Ian?" The house stays dead silent.

Silence rings throughout the house, with only the sound of my laboured breathing filling the white noise surrounding me. "Mom?" I'd like to think they're playing one of those jump scare games on me and Ian didn't murder her in cold blood. "Ian?" I knock on his bedroom door, "Where's mom?" All of the vessels in my body detach from their ascribed organs when my ears perceive a muffled voice contending to let out an audible noise from behind the door. "Ian!" I quickly twist the doorknob.

Laid down on his stomach near his bed with polypropylene ropes suppressing his arms and legs behind his back and a black silicone ball gag crammed into his mouth, I quickly take in the abhorrence etched in his tear-rimmed eyes.

Just before I could rush to help him out of the ropes, my lungs convulse, and a crashing *BANG* of metal fills the room. My body collapses forward, and I pass out.

3

"ARE YOU ALRIGHT, LOVE?" I hear Ian ask.

"I have a headache."

"I know you do." He replies before turning around in his swivel chair. "Your scalp is injured. I… I closed the wound for… for you."

"Wait," I falter, "what happened last night? Why did she tie you up and why did she knock me unconscious?"

"You were dreaming."

I know I wasn't dreaming. "Stop right there. That was not a fucking dream, Ian. Stop changing the subject, please. Tell me what is going on."

"I will tell you when I come back." He stands up and proceeds to bond the black buttons of his blue flannel shirt into their holes. "Stay in here. I'll be back shortly."

Perhaps since he tends to be attention deficit and a scatter mouth when it comes to conversations like this, he'll less likely want to tell me anything when he comes back. "Where are you going?"

"To a pharmacy, because your headache will get worse throughout the day if you don't take an analgesic." Before shutting the door behind him and leaving me to myself, he requests, "Lock the door, please."

———

I listen to mom's voice bickering with someone other than Teddie and causing a kerfuffle downstairs.

Reminding me of the one too many times we've gotten into shouting matches, and she would sometimes threaten me, and I usually went running to my dad because he was always on my side.

She's not the best person when she wants to slit someone's throat, maybe even her own, with a kitchen knife.

I know my brother instructed me not to leave the room earlier, but I rise from beneath the bed covers and rebel; settling myself at the mount of the staircase.

"How long has it been since you took them away from her to claim as your own?" He enquires.

31

"That doesn't matter! You want them to know the truth so bad, go hang yourself. Until I see a report that you and your cousin are deceased, I won't be telling them a damn thing."

"They hate you as their mother anyway."

THWACK "Ask your bitch son if he really does. Oh, right…" She adds, "You're a deadbeat to him."

We already know that she keeps just about everything from us. What could possibly be so complicated that she feels the need to hide from her own children?

"DON'T ever hit me again, bitch! I raised him better than you ever could! You left me to do all the work, all you did was sit on your ass!"

A painful headache begins to overtake my head, and it feels like the blade of a sharpened screwdriver is cleaving my temples. It proceeds to spread throughout my head, desperate for medication. "Where the hell is he?"

The house is silent once again after the bickering recedes and whomever mom was raising her voice at, makes a rather quick exit. I dart down the steps and into the kitchen to fetch myself a towering glass of cold water.

"You were listening in, weren't you?" It's mom.

I take a gulp of water from my glass cup before answering, "Oh, to you screaming and slapping Cole? Maybe, I heard some of it. You really don't tell us shit, do you? All you do is lie and keep secrets."

"Some secrets," She murmurs.

"Some secrets?" More like an entire mining shaft, and we're the miners. "Some secrets! What were you and Cole arguing about? If that's not a secret, you can tell me! Joselyn?"

I at least expect a sentence or two to come out of her mouth, but she stays in her seat behind the counter, with her lips pursed together and a thwarted look in her eyes. She finally parts her lips, "I can't. It's nothing important."

"I know. It's all you do. You told him to go kill himself for fuck's sake, then you'll tell Ian and me what we want to know. You are devious." Ian needs to slap the words of Jesus into her. A decent parent wouldn't lie and keep secrets from their own children.

"It's not my job to be telling you what you want to know."

34

"Then whose is it?" Before she can come up with an answer, probably an ambiguous answer, to my question, the alarm system chimes. Ian paces into the kitchen clutching onto a couple of grocery bags and shaking out the snow flurries that have alighted onto the dark bangs of his hair. I smirk, "Welcome back. Mom has something to tell you."

"Do me a favour and go set yourself on fire," She snarls. "Please, Raelynn."

"Jesus Christ, Joselyn! Watch your damn mouth, please, that's your daughter you're threatening! Go set your own damn self on fire!"

"That's mom to you, sir!"

"No, it's okay," I assure. "She'll be plummeting to hell soon anyway. Come talk to me when you're done, Ian."

———

"For all I know, you could be giving me Rohypnol."

"I wouldn't give you Rohypnol even if somebody promised me to tell me where my father is. I swear it's Ibuprofen."

I blink at him.

He adds, "Look, I know I fucked up the first time, and I apologize for being a dick and raping you. I promise you this is nothing but Ibuprofen… I don't have access to any illegal drugs. If you would like to see the bottle it came from, I can show y—"

"No," I smile with my lips, "you've convinced me." I guess this is some sort of peace offering from him to me since he's come to realize he has wronged me. I will probably never be able to see him as I once did.

He displays a couple of white, round tablets in his palm for me to take. "What did mom want to tell me?"

"I'll tell you what happened while you were gone if you promise to tell me what happened last night."

The only reason I didn't just confront her about knocking me unconscious is that I know her too well and she'd try to weakly convince me that she didn't do it, or she'd quickly brush off the accusation.

"Fine. I..." Before he could even come forward with the first few words, we both hear mom call him from downstairs.

"WHAT?" He rolls his eyes. "I'll be back…"

4

"CAN YOU PLEASE TELL THE truth for once! Did you switch them… that's all I'm asking! Not going to answer the question? That's okay because I already know you're lying to me and you did it."

Ian sounds angry, almost as if he's yelling at mom. But for what this time?

My brother pushes open the door with his back with ease, holding a plate almost overlaid with food in one hand and a water-filled glass cup in his other; his eyes appear puffy and chafe as if he's been crying. "Have you… brushed your teeth yet?" The flow of his voice suddenly cracks. He has been crying.

"I… I just woke up," I answer.

"Okay." He sets the dishes down on the nightstand beside my bed before turning around to leave.

"Ian?" I catch him before he leaves the doorway. He rests his left hand against the door frame, stops in his tracks, then looks down at his feet. He answers with a slightly concerned, "Hm?"

"What's wrong?"

"Nothing's wrong," The guy lets out a sigh, simply dismissing a proper answer to my question, "I'm okay."

"Are you sure?"

"Yes."

———

I don't remember getting into my bed or telling Ian about Cole—if that is what he's so upset about. And he never told me about what happened the night before.

After scarfing down the plate full of breakfast and downing the entire glass of water in less than 20 minutes, I hop out of my comfort zone with the dishes in hands and open the door to the voice of my brother competing in a screaming match against our mother, in the kitchen. I sigh. It's nothing new.

I was surprised upon discovering they also have a strained mother-child relationship when I first got here.

"I own this damn house, you just live here! I cook, I clean, I pay the bills, and I baby your grown ass because you're too lazy to take care of yourself! No wonder dad left you!"

The house-rattling sound of something heavy being thrown against a wall forces me to scurry myself down the staircase for the source. Wielding a meat knife in her right and clutching my brother by his throat with her left, she restrains him against a wall in the lounge; threatening his existence. "Mom…" I intervene, "let him go. Leave him alone."

Reluctant to my request, she waves the knife close to his face, "Your father disowned you." She growls. "I brought you into this world, and I can take you out. You're living in my fucking house. If you don't like it here, kill yourself or grab your shit and get the fuck out."

SMASH, *CLINK*, "I SAID LEAVE HIM ALONE!" Her long hair snags most of the now scattered shards of the cup I tossed at her back. She releases her grip on his throat, then twists her head around with an arduous look in her eyes at me—like when a hungry owl spots its prey. "You BITCH."

The woman charges me. I quickly hoist my plate over my head as if it were an apsis shield, and it barely deflects the blade of her meat cleaver.

"LEAVE HER ALONE!" Ian exclaims.

The knife dives in for a second blow, desperate for bloodshed. My plate-shield deflects it once again, forcing the weapon to fling backwards from her grip.

His arms clasps around her abdomen before she is able to turn her back to retrieve her weapon. "Open the door!" He directs me, and I immediately sprint towards the nearest door and twist and pull its knob.

"PUT ME DOWN, YOU F—!" With her hands, she hassles to pry herself free from Ian's arms as he hauls her outside with a stable posture.

"Stay right there! When you calm down and stop acting like a fucking seven-year-old brat, we'll let you back in!"

This is how she always was for the both of us; we're used to it. And we both used to run to our dads whenever her tantrums flared. Not much was done, probably because they were afraid of her menacing anger issue as well. "I'm sorry." I remove the swing lid of the garbage can in the kitchen, break out the manual broom and dustpan aside the pantry, then begin to sweep up the prickly disaster I've created on the floor in the lounge.

"You don't have proper shoes on. I'll clean it up, you go back to your room."

"You really love to be alone with your thoughts," I affirm, "I'm not going to my room. I want to talk to you."

"About what?"

"I want to know why you've been so upset recently."

He takes the broom from my hands before replying to my question with one of his famous answers, "Life."

I purse my lips together. Is there anything else going on in his life other than family issues? "What else is going on?"

He turns his head to glare at me for a second. "And you called me nosy. Look at yourself. Just stuff that really doesn't matter."

The little voice embedded in the farthermost part of my mind attempts to repel me from asking him more questions. I neglect its pleas, "Stuff...?"

"Jesus, Raelynn," He rolls his eyes, "I begged my dad for a younger sibling when I was a little boy, and now I already hate having one when I've only had you for almost one. You're so damn nosy. You want to know, it's complicated stuff. Stuff you... you wouldn't understand."

"And I've been asking for an older brother since grade six. I'm still listening. How do you know I wouldn't understand them? Life has taught me its lessons plenty of times before."

"I can tell you're the social butterfly type. You're not used to being a lone wolf and keeping things to yourself, that's what I mean."

"I can't really relate." But I can try to relate.

"Exactly. Nobody stops to flip through the pages of a book about something they can't relate to. Not anymore anyway."

"Well," I settle myself up onto the back cushion of the couch, "can you give me a brief summary of your book so I can try to understand. I've been around the same people in my life so far, I need something new."

He grins, "You're interested? Sure. I hate our own mother, everybody hates me, and I hate myself, just not as much as you and the world does."

"Uh, I... I don't hate you..." I pout, "I'm not sure where you got that from."

"You act as if you hate me because I hurt you, and I can't blame you for it."

"Why do you think I do? Why do you hate yourself?"

He parts his lips a bit like he wants to respond to my question, but then shakes his head and proceeds to sweep the shards into the dustpan. "Never mind."

"If you got that from mom, you know she's crazy, and she doesn't mean most of the things she says. I don't, nobody hates you, Ian."

"No, I didn't get it from her. You don't know me personally, so you can't say so. Thank you for trying to make me feel better."

"Tell me more… please." Aside from being bullied and neglected by mom at home, he was bullied in school as well and had anonymous people calling him an accident and a mistake and a fuck up most of his adolescent life. Just like a lot of people who have been through long-term abuse and bullying, these people have got to his head and polluted his mind with toxic thoughts.

To finally distract me and drive my attention away from inquiring him about a possibly even worse or a significant part of his life—his time at the university he attended—, he mentions something we almost completely forgot about. Mom is still outside. "She's scarily quiet out there."

"Are you sure she's not thinking about resilience and how she was just about to murder us with the cleaver?" I ask as he goes to store the broom and dustpan back into their corner next to the pantry.

"Likely ever the case," He chuckles, "she never thinks about anything."

"Go check on her."

He goes to take a peek through the door blinds be-fore opening the door and stepping out onto the veran-da, "She's gone."

"You're shitting me."

"I wouldn't. She's really gone."

———

"This isn't the first time she has run off without any indication of where." Our aunt Teddie, I mean officer Niles, tilts her stetson. "Don't worry, we'll conduct a search."

It doesn't make sense. We're not the abusive ones, she is.

5

"YOU REALLY DON'T GIVE A fuck about mom, do
you?" I ask him.

He sighs, keeping his eyes glued to the pages of his
book. "No, I don't care. Nobody gives a single fuck
about her. Can we blame ourselves? She doesn't care
about us, why should we care about her?"

"She's our mother, you're supposed to care. You're
not rereading one of my books, are you?"

His face suddenly surges with blood, turning his face
red. He bites his lip, "Yes…"

"I see." I was hoping he wouldn't lie. "How are you reading without your glasses?"

"I have prescribed contacts. Where are you going anyway?"

"Uh…" I'm not sure if I should lie or tell him where I'm actually going, I wouldn't just be going outside with my purse and keys. When I decide on answering, "Somewhere," he sets the book down on it's back and pulls something out of one of the pockets of his jeans; my phone. "You can tell me where, if you want this back."

"Dick."

"Thank you. Go on, tell me, little sis."

"Jesus, why do you always have to coerce me, Ian! Fine, " I confess, "I'm going to Charlottetown."

"That's three hours away. For what?"

I had a feeling he was going to ask that. "I'm just going to talk to Shane's mother. His parents, if his dad decides to tag."

He smiles, not with a regular smile, a delighted smile portraying heinousness on his lips. "You better hope that chickenshit doesn't tag along, she needs a life-long break from him anyway. Can I come with you, please?"

I shrug at his request, "I don't know what it is you have against Shane, but I promise you he's a great guy... sometimes his dad is nice. Yes, you can come." I wonder if it's because he's merely my boyfriend and brothers and fathers are naturally inclined to dislike the guys their sisters and daughters bring home. Or maybe, he knows something about him that I have yet to discover.

———

You'd assume Shane's mother, Megan is other than his biological mother due to their opposing features.

The only feature Shane shares with his mother is amber freckles stippling the irises of his dark brown eyes like the wings of a monarch. She has full amber eyes, and they light up when she sees us.

 6

"OH HELL NO, YOU ARE not…" I furrow my brows, "stop taking pictures of me, or I'll break that fucking camera." *Click* I hear the faint sound producing from Ian's Canon camera after every couple of minutes. "Ian…"

"I'm almost done."

"What the fuck! Stop, you're creepy!" I don't know what it is that makes him think otherwise. I quickly extend both of my arms out in front of me, forcing large droplets of foamy water to plunge out from the tub onto the tiled floor in front of him. "Get out!"

"Hey, hey," He chides, "okay, I'll stop." He suddenly grins smugly, "Only if you let me join in."

"No."

"You know you're a mean little devil. I bet you were way meaner when you were a little girl."

"I'm a little devil? Or are you implying that because I'm too assertive for you?"

He squints his eyes slightly at me before asking, "What do you mean?"

"You know what I mean. You just called me a mean little devil for saying no. Just because I'm not as submissive as you'd like me to be, that doesn't mean I'm a little devil. It's called having self-respect, and I don't want you in this tub with me, neither do I want you taking crude photos."

"I didn't mean it in that way. I'm calling you a mean little devil overall because you're little in size and you're a mean little girl." He implies, his expression softening.

"After I saved your ass from the literal devil." Or was it the other way around and Ian made her try to kill us to make her still seem like the dysfunctional one.

I can't leap down to conclusions because I've lived in the same house with mom before college and she's always gone cuckoo whenever her anger flared, but Ian is a bizarre book filled with questionable things; he's an unsympathetic person, and I wouldn't be shocked to discover she went crazy that day because of him.

"You did save me from her."

I'm not taking it as a direct compliment. "Okay…"

"I'm still getting in with you. Or one of these days I will."

"No, the hell you aren't." I clutch onto the rim of the tub before adding, "In fact, I was just about to get out. So you can leave now, please." Ian stays standing in his place with his camera aside him like a statue, silently analyzing me through the lenses of his blue-framed eyeglasses. "Are you going to leave?" I ask, annoyed.

"No."

"Screw you then." It's abuse. And I bet mom is a reason he's like this—if it's not that his father raised him the wrong way, which is most likely the case.

"Have you been bullied?"

"About what?"

"Your weight."

I'm healthy, and I was born a bigger size, but a lot of people just see fat and not me. Yes, I have been bullied, but why does he want to know? I purse my lips, then slightly part them, "No. Why are you asking these weird ass questions?"

"You're hesitant to be naked in front of me."

"I'm your fucking sister, not your damn mistress! I'm hesitant because I can't trust you anymore!" After he decided it was okay to rape me, attempt to change the subject when I confronted him about it, and half-ass his apology to me.

"Hmph," With a sudden defeated look in his eyes, he nods, then responds, "I'm not surprised."

"Can you leave now?"

"Sure."

———

"IAN DAUGHTRY!" Strokes of neon blue high-lighter streaks over sentences in passages of my book. I'll kill him. "Did you highlight in my book?" No an-swer. I stand up. "Ian!" His room is right down the hallway from mine, so he should be able to hear me. I push open the door to his room, not finding him in it, but a painting canvas and a polaroid vector set aside each other on the floor beside his bed. "Shit…"

The sun is just starting to hide behind the trees, so I doubt he'd be outside while it's getting dark.

"Yes, Raelynn?" I hear his voice ask from at least ten feet down the hall behind me, followed by the sound of the balcony door being shut slowly. So he was outside.

60

I twist around. "I hate when you disappear on me like that." Well, now I do. "Did you highlight in my book?" He was reading it yesterday. He forgot all about it when we came back, and I picked it up to put it back in my room, didn't see a blue highlighter in sight.

He raises an eyebrow. "No, I never highlighted in a book."

"Are you lying to me?"

"No." He assures. "I don't use highlighters. You'd catch me using a pen."

"Pants on fire. You're the last person who had the book. I would never damage a book."

"Well," He blinks, "if you would like to find your book vandalizing culprit, ask the woman who thought it would be nice to set my Bible on fire because I wouldn't vandalize a book either."

"She what…" Maybe she is the demon he was talking about.

"What?"

'You're so ADD."

"Thank you, ma'am. I know I am." He suddenly lowers his eyes from mine, and his grasp around his plastic paint cups compresses before he makes a beeline back to his room.

Why so quickly? I let out a sigh. Why am I not surprised about her vandalizing my book? But I wouldn't be surprised if he did it either and he's just blaming her to stay out of trouble. "Ian?"

"What?" He replies.

"Answer this for me, please. Why were you yelling at mom the other morning?" I don't expect him to proceed with the direct reason why, but it's better to know something valid than to know nothing, and jumping to conclusions.

Behind the creviced door, the guy hesitates for a split-second. "Do I have to answer that?"

"Answer honestly."

In the chillingly passive tone of voice he uses when speaking on unsettling subjects, he answers with, "Because she drugged you."

My jaw hangs. And before I could clench it back into place, he asks, "Can you remember anything before waking up the following morning after I gave you those pills?"

"I don't… know." I was about to tell him that mom was arguing with his father at least half an hour before he got back, and he was about to tell me about that sick mania I walked in on before getting knocked unconscious the previous night. "I…"

"No, of course, you don't remember anything."

"YOU GAVE ME THE FUCKING PILLS!"

"I did, but I didn't notice they were switched, I couldn't have. Those weren't the Ibuprofen I brought. She switched them."

"So how do you know they weren't Ibuprofen if you didn't notice she switched them?"

"You fell drowsy before we could even tell each other anything. It's not supposed to make you drowsy."

If she were here right now, she'd pretend like she's done absolutely nothing wrong because she loves to be trifling. "What the fuck…" I push open his room door, "why didn't you tell me any of this sooner?"

Settled on the floor, canvas in lap and a small paintbrush in hand with the polaroid, the paint cups, and a cup full of water set in front of him, it's obvious he got himself settled in his comfort zone just in case I'd start asking too many questions. With a clear frown across his face, he answers, "I hurt you already, and I apologized for it. So what makes you think I'd take the blame for her actions and cause you to resent me more?"

"Then don't take the blame for her."

"It's not as easy as you think." He drops his paint-brush into the cup of water. "You don't trust me, and you don't trust mom either. In your mind, and be honest about this, if you were to discover you were drugged without me telling you, who would you come after first?"

"You."

"Why?"

"Because you raped me. And after waking up from being sedated, only bits and pieces are left to be recollected."

"Exactly."

She's conducting her own twisted mind games, and we're her subjects. Almost as if she's trying to distract us with each other so we can't pay attention to her.

66

I'm glad he told me this before she could carry out her plan to blame everything wrong that happens on him and get us to turn against each other.

"So, now that the bitch is nowhere in sight or even in this house… what was it that you wanted to tell me?" He asks with general curiosity in his voice.

I take a baby step back towards the door, in case he decides to raise Satan up from the depths of hell because Cole left without thinking twice. "Uh…" I falter, "you tell me yours first."

"Joselyn knocked you unconscious."

"I know she did, I mean before that. You were tied up."

He grabs onto the handle of his paintbrush before responding with, "That was nothing."

"So you expect me to tell you what happened while you were gone, but you can't tell me why..." He's on my last nerve with his stubbornness. "Look, I don't know what you're trying to hide from me, but we really need to talk about the secret keeping."

"Why?" He inquires dumbly.

"Because first its mom hoarding a million secrets, and now it's you. We don't need that. Keeping secrets won't make anything better, if anything, it makes the situation worse. No matter how good or bad this secret or secrets are, I want to know, not because I'm nosy, but because I care about you. And if there's something much more dangerous going on between you and her, you need to let me or Teddie know, like right now. Children aren't the only subjects to abuse."

"Hmph." He grunts. "What if I'm not ready to tell you? Why do you care anyway?"

I glare, "What? What do you mean? I care because now I know something is going on with you."

"I don't like talking."

"Then you'll end up like mom. It's been how many years, and she still won't tell us why our dads suddenly disappeared on us, not only that, a heap of other secrets." Painful silence overtakes the gap between Ian and I, and then the rest of the room almost immediately, while he squints his eyes into a stinging scowl at me for offending him. "You promised me!"

"I did, but that doesn't guarantee I will actually tell you."

"Why not? What is so secretive about it?"

"Nothing," He growls, gritting his teeth, "don't fucking worry about it, Raelynn. I don't see why you would give so much of a fuck about me when you're probably secretly wishing I'd just die already. I'm done talking. Get out."

7

"WHERE ARE YOU GOING?" I hear his voice behind me.

"Don't worry about it." I brush off his question, because I know if I tell him where I'm going, he will snap.

"Hey," He abruptly raises his tone, "you didn't answer my question!"

I clench my right hand into an ireful fist. "None of your damn business, Ian!" I bark. "You hurt me, and now you have the nerve to ask me why I'm leaving. You've been influenced by mom or something else malevolent bec—"

"Where will you go? You know Shane doesn't even give a fuck about you, you don't know where your father is. This is your only sanctuary, and I can prove it. If only you'd shut your trap and listen to me, I'd tell you. I'm not letting you leave."

"So, now you're making excuses for everything you've done to me. The only thing you have proven to me is that you're a psychotic control freak, and you're jealous."

"I'm not making excuses, I know what I've done wrong, and I apologized to you. This isn't about that." He lets out a slightly exhausted sigh. "What is there to be jealous about? Shane isn't the best person for you, sweetie."

"And you aren't either. What is it that you need to tell me?"

As if I just made the right point he's been yearning for me to get to, he quickly presses his hands together before answering, "Finally. Will you please listen to me?"

"Sure." I roll my eyes.

"I went through your texts with him because…"

As he proceeds to drill into his plausibly deceiving reasons and unfurl his collected evidence from yearbooks, pictures, screenshots, and his computer for me, I begin to open my eyes to what he's been trying to warn me about. "After graduation, I got my revenge on him. His father has been sending me threatening texts ever since. I still haven't unblocked his number."

The most haunting, but an authentic piece of evidence is a yearbook picture of his high school's track team the year he was on it; I remember what happened that afternoon like the back of my hand.

I didn't attend the same school as him, I was on my high school's volleyball team, and we had a set against his school that afternoon.

We were all in the cafeteria doing homework before we were supposed to start and first, a girl came in and asked them for a quick photo for the yearbook. She took the picture and left.

Next thing I knew, I looked up from where I was sitting, three guys—who looked robust for their ages, were blustering this scrawny boy at the table near us, and nobody went to help him.

So when they began to assault him, everybody stood up, some even started filming. I ripped my earphones out of my ears and attempted to break up the fight until one of the guys, with a firm hand, jerked me away and knocked me down onto the floor. "That was you?!"

"What was me?" He raises his eyebrows.

Pointing to the picture, I reply with, "There. You don't remember what happened that day, do you?"

"I try not to."

I know it's painful for him. "He hurt you, and I skipped my game for you."

"And you kissed me."

I have to admit that I did give him a smooch on the cheek because I felt terrible for him.

Our coaches lugged them away from the boy. He laid nearly unconscious, fresh bruises emerging all over his face, chest, and arms.

The merciless expressions on their faces signifying "he totally deserved it" as they were forced to leave the room in the hands of administration repulsed me. But the fact that no one even cared enough to help him in the first place sickened me even more.

I had to beg my coach to let me skip the big game to spend the remainder of the afternoon with him until his dad arrived to pick him up.

It's now a haunting memory. I hang my head, "I'm so sorry, Ian." I've been so stubborn all this time.

"It's okay," He bites his bottom lip, "I understand why you thought I was jealous, I'm sorry. If you decide to break up with him, tell him you heard it from me. I don't think he knows you're my sister, yet."

"Why wouldn't I?"

"You seem so devoted to him."

"Yeah, well not anymore. Now that you've shown me him between then and now, he hasn't changed, and I don't condone people like him."

"That's not surprising, even after I gave him a taste of his own medicine." He closes his yearbook. "He's been targeting me since kindergarten, and now he's moved on to you, and I'm sure others as well since I'm not there to be a personal punching bag for him and his friends.

I take a big step back. "What?" I squint my eyes slightly, "He's not —"

77

"I know how he treats you, Raelynn. It's far from how your dad did, he would be disappointed in you to learn you're dating somebody like Shane. I know I'm not your father, and I shouldn't be telling you who to date, but if you were a little more experienced in dating, out of all people, you wouldn't be dating him. If you don't condone people like him, why are you dating him?"

He's right. He would be kind of disappointed in me, and I probably wouldn't have had enough headspace to listen to him and would've thought he was just an over-protective dad.

"No," He asserts, taking notice of the tears brimming my eyes, "no. Don't look at me like that. You know he's lying when he says he loves you, it's not surprising. You're only still with him because you want to feel loved, or maybe some other reason."

"You couldn't put it in a less hurtful way?"

"I'm sorry —"

"YOU'RE NOT FUCKING SORRY! STOP SAY-
ING THAT!"

"So now you're mad at me for being honest? I
wouldn't lie to you."

Frustration and enmity and hopelessness over-
whelms me for a moment. Infuriated with the heart-
shattering truth about Shane, and also with Ian's explic-
it honesty, I chuck one of my shoes at him.

He snags it before it could hit him. "Excuse you!"
He flares. "Calm down, please. I know you're angry."

"You could've just lied to me like you always do!"
Some things are meant to be left unsaid.

"I don't lie to you, sweetie. Take it as me trying to
keep certain things from getting into your head. And
that my dear, needed to be said before you get traumati-
cally hurt."

I attempt to chuck another one of my shoes at him.

"No, stop it, put it down. You're not a child, act like
Raelynn. I understand how upset you are." He extends
his arms out towards me, "Come here. Give me a hug."

8

"MOM!" I'M NOT SURE WHICH situation is worse; one of her outbursts of rage or finding her standing in the doorway watching us after disappearing for a few days.

"I hate both of you." She mutters before leaving the doorway.

"YOU TRIFLING BITCH... WHERE HAVE YOU BEEN?!"

She evokes Ian's nerves. "Don't walk away from me..."

"Ian... no," I falter, "she's only stirring the pot."

"And I'm spilling the potion. You stay in here."

I already know what's about to happen. "How did she even get in any way?" I let out before he leaves the room.

He lets his head drop, before letting out a quiet sigh. "Don't worry about it. Just worry about a plan for breaking up with Shane, if you haven't already."

What else does he know that I don't?

I grab my phone off of my nightstand, hesitant of dialling my now ex-boyfriend's number while a quarrel is amplifying downstairs. It rings four times before sending me to voicemail. "Shit…" I cuss to myself.

If Ontario were to be a little bit closer to this province, I would keep my foot on the gas for a little more than a few hours to call our relationship off in person.

I roll out from beneath the duvet onto the floor, pick myself up to scurry on my runners, then grab the key to my car.

———

If I can't reach Shane, I know the person who would send a message to him for me. "Megan, is your husband home right now?"

She shakes her head, "You missed him. He left an hour ago."

"Okay," I exhale, "um… I need to talk to Shane, and he didn't pick up his pho—"

As if she already knew I was going to show up to tell her this, she immediately raises one of her hands to finish my explanation, "You're breaking up with him, aren't you?"

My eyes dilate with awe. "H—How do... you know?"

A smile suddenly broadens weakly across her face before releasing a slight chuckle, "I know your brother well. I knew he'd tell you about his ordeal with Shane. I'll send him the message."

"Wow... okay. Thank you so much."

"You're welcome."

I don't think Shane would be excited to hear the bad news, (good news for me), from his mother.

———

"Ian!" I call out as soon as I walk into the front door. "Ian… mom?" I shouldn't have left them with each other. They fight like piranhas.

I lower my head to catch on the floor splotches of red spotting the hardwood just beneath my shoes. "Shit…"

I proceed behind the crimson trail to its dead end, centring the kitchen floor where a santoku knife with a red blade lies gazing back at me.

I climb the staircase a couple of steps a time.

The door of his bedroom was left halfway open, and when I push it open, my heart plunges from its arteries.

My brother sits up against the frame of his bed motionless and cold to the touch, with a syringe piercing a canal in his left arm.

———

"Heroin overdose. Has he shown any signs of possible addiction or mental health problems?"

"I… don't know." There are only two questions on my mind. Why didn't he tell me anything after I offered to help him and where or who was he able to obtain heroin through?

If both heroin and Rohypnol are illegal, and Ian had both, then he must have a dealer (or dealers). Now he's gotten himself into a coma, and if anything, it may be too late to derive solid answers.

"Now is not the time to cause more havoc. You broke up with Shane without giving him a reason, now he's mad at you, and your brother's in critical condition. What happened before you found Ian?"

"I left to go to Prince Edward Island to talk to Shane's mother."

"So, Ian instructed you to break up with him? Why? What else?"

"They have years of tension between each other, and Ian's been trying to tell me that Shane wants to hurt me and I didn't believe him." I clench my hand. "Mom unexpectedly showed up in the house, I don't know if she has a key or she broke in, but neither of us let her in. I left to go talk to Shane's mom, went straight back, then not only found Ian, but a knife covered in blood on the kitchen floor as well."

Mental health, not something many people pay attention to when someone harms others and themselves. Even I've never thought about it, I merely call someone an asshole and evil based on how bad their actions are. It definitely doesn't excuse them for their self-destructive behaviour, but it is a source to look for in its presence. Otherwise, if mental illness isn't present, they need aid in being a better person.

It's kind of more about self-esteem than mental health, solely. A lot of these people are good at loathing themselves and summoning that pain onto others. Some may fail to just acknowledge they're causing damage.

In Ian's case, I'm not him, so I can't be directly accurate, but I know one is probably self-loathe so severe that he's turned to drugs to numb his sorrows. And even though he's done some horrible things to me, it hurts my heart seeing him at his lowest.

9

WHILE TEDDIE IS ACCUMULATING DNA on the forensic evidence from a fellow team of investigators, I've been prohibited from entering the house—that is unsurprisingly in Ian's name and not mom's—and from seeing my brother; so I am forced to stay with her until the investigation is finished and my brother fully recovers.

Receiving a text from someone I know—and might still trust because Ian's supported claims about Shane made me start questioning the motives of everyone I know—my phone's screen illuminates.

'What happened to your brother?'

Apperceiving that I haven't spoken about Ian or to anyone since the mishap, I balk, squinting my eyes at the screen as if he just asked me the answer to a complicated math problem. 'Don't worry about it.'

'I can't not worry.'

How does he know he's my brother? I've never let out about that either.

The only person who needs to be informed about Ian right now is Cole. And even though Teddie addressed me earnestly about leaving my only safe spot, I have to go to tell him if nobody else will before it's too late.

He works at a pharmacy in Charlottetown, and the only reason I know that is because of Megan, but she told me not to tell Ian.

———

I find it ironic how the sky continues to be its standard blissful blue after these past morbid weeks; not intending to mean personifying would be more appropriate.

Behind the counter, a guy in a white coat with honey blonde hair bound into a hasty ponytail stands while providing undivided attention to the pages of a book in his hand. Not wanting to lose his place in the middle of a passage, he doesn't look away from it, but asks, "May I help you?"

"Yes," I sneer, "I'm here for my Rohypnol prescription."

"What Rohypnol?" He disrupts his attention from the book to me, his swallowtail gold eyes dilate, "We don't —... Kimbe—, I'm sorry, Raelynn?"

"Correct. How do you know?"

"Cole, " He calls, "your daughter's here, and she's asking for a Rohypnol prescription."

What? I'm not his daughter.

"You sure? We don't carry or prescribe Flunitrazepam. It's ill—, oh… hi, Raelynn. You're here for… Rohypnol?"

Maybe he's in good spirits now, but I can see behind those morpho blue eyes that he's exhausted and Ian is one of possibly hundred things that produce great strain on him. My lips sink back down into a frown. "No, definitely no, I was kidding. I was looking for you, Cole. I don't need anything, it's Ian. He's in the hospital in Halifax because of a heroin overdose, and you need to see him, right now. He woke up from the coma, and he's starting to move a bit more, and he's able to talk, according to the updates I've been getting, but I haven't been able to check on him since last week."

———

I know Ian will get on my ass for lying to him as soon as he gets out.

At least an hour outside of Nova Scotia, I receive a call from Teddie, with an unusual stern tone in her voice, asking me where I am. Oh shit. "Baie Verde. I'll be there in another hour or two." DNA has been divulged.

"Where were you?"

"Prince Edward. I... went to see Cole."

She slowly purses her lips before releasing them to ask, "Told him about Ian?"

"Yes." She's not usually as serious as she has been these past weeks, and that's what scares me.

"Okay. I want you to identify one person for me." Out from a sheet of paper sized clasp envelope, she takes out a paper with a red-capped tube attached to it. And inside of the red-capped tube displays a cotton swab with one tip saturated with blood. "Do you know Kyle Garrett? I'm sure you do since you were dating Shane. This is his blood. And..." She pulls out another paper from the envelope, with the bloody knife I found in a large ziplock bag attached to it, "Ian and Joselyn's fingerprints were found on the handle of the knife..." Last paper, with the syringe in a ziplock, "well over 15 millilitres of liquid heroin was injected into Ian, and no DNA or fingerprints were found on the outside of it except for his skin cells in the tip of the needle."

I'm at a loss for words, and we can't see or even fucking talk to my brother probably for another week, so we are unable to get the proper answers for what initially happened, and it gives the runners time to cover their asses and wreak more havoc. "Wh— what… what the hell?"

Is this what Ian was trying to warn me about, but I refused to believe him?

"Y'all want to charge them for trespassing?" She asks.

"If we can find them, that's up to Ian." I know someone who will tell me where Kyle and Joselyn are if I intimidate him hard enough. But I know Teddie, and even Ian, wouldn't be happy to find out I took a risk to get my hands on well-needed information.

 IO

"I DIDN'T DO IT."

Without us telling anybody we know—Cole is an exception, there's already a petty rumour going around that Ian attempted suicide. It's now a petty rumour because we're currently learning he, in fact, didn't inject himself with the 15 millilitres of heroin. "Since nobody else is here to clarify their side of what happened, you're our main source for this investigation. I need you to clarify before you leave."

Suppressing a confused expression on his face, he explains his perspective to Teddie with an apathetic tone in his voice as if he's not in shock at all from his near death experience and he was expecting it to happen. Observing the subtle movement of his eyes, he's keeping something back.

Maybe he distracted me with breaking up with Shane so I wouldn't get hurt.

"Keep an eye on your brother... and for God's sake, don't leave him alone."

I definitely won't be making that fatal mistake again. "I won't."

As dangerous as it can be now, he will eventually, if not immediately, assure me that I don't have to keep an eye on him and he's able to take care of himself. "Here," I pass a change of clothes to him, "go change."

"Okay..." He presents a sly smile with his lips at me before standing up then peeling the gown off of himself. And before he could expose his member down there purposely for me to see, I swiftly raise my phone close in front of my eyes, "NOT IN FRONT OF ME DAMMIT! You are sick!"

"Then don't look. But you can look at this…"

"If it's your dick, no thanks."

"Not that. My rib cage."

"Did you do that on yourself? I've never noticed that." Etched into the thin skin of his left rib cage in black and watercolour pigmented ink, a speckled, hallow silhouette of a dragon serpentines transversely; the spade of its arrow-like tail ending narrowly above his pelvic bone.

"I drew it, and I got it tattooed... for someone."

"It's pretty, I like it."

The corners of his lips curve up. And just as he's about to respond with "thank you," we hear a couple of soft, barely audible knocks on the door. I grasp the metal handle but don't turn it until he's fully dressed.

In sheer repulsion, Ian rolls his eyes, then turns his head in the other direction; immediately upon laying his eyes on the person.

"Ian," I let out an anxious chuckle, "why are you so mean? At least say hi." This person is one of my good friends, Jayden Cline—also known as Dr. Cline. "I'm sorry. He's been a little… grumpy lately."

"No, it's okay," He smiles, "I see he's still the same shelled tortoise."

"Oh no… high school?"

"University."

Either he's naturally inclined to dislike people I know or something horrible happened between them, and Ian is stubborn enough to hold a timeless grudge. "Jayden is going to make sure it's okay for you to leave."

"He is not touching me." He asserts in a bitter tone with his head still turned.

"He's not going to hurt you."

"I don't care."

Shortly convinced of the idea that he wouldn't go berserk on the doctor that took care of him, I quickly realize that I am dead wrong.

In my mind, I plead for him to stay calm.

He doesn't turn his head to look at him. But as soon as Jayden even lifts a finger at him, he snatches him by the wrist and finally snaps his head in his direction with a blazing inferno in his eyes. "TOUCH ME, and I will SHATTER your fucking arm!"

"IAN! LET HIM GO!" I compel. But instead of listening to me, he keeps Jayden's arm at compliance, tears in his eyes threatening to spill over. "What the hell is wrong with you?!"

Staying impassive and quiet, as if he knows why Ian is acting so aggressive towards him, he turns his head towards me and his voice quivers, "Uh… he's uhh… it's okay, he's just… tense?"

He releases his grip on his wrist. "We don't need your help. Stay the fuck away from me and my family! Get out!"

He lays that same hand on my shoulder before exiting the room. "What the fuck, Ian?"

"Raelynn! Can we just fucking leave? Now?"

"NO! You need to apologize to him!"

"I don't need to apologize to ANYBODY! Look…" Wiping away the remaining tear trails from his cheeks, he gains the courage to look me in the eyes, "I'm sorry. I'm fucking sorry, okay? I'm tired of saying it to people who don't deserve an apology."

"What do you mean?" I ask. "You just threatened somebody who took care of you, the reason you're still alive and talking to me right now! And he texted me

worrying about you, of course, he deserves an
apology!"

" I don't give a fuck, he doesn't deserve any type of
apology from me. You don't understand, it's not surprising. If anything, he should've let me fucking die, I wish
he would've so I wouldn't have had to wake up to see his
face years later. Can we go home now, please?"

"Ian! Stop it. You don't mean any of that."

"I do. I know you think this is some pointless dis-
agreement, but it's not. I will never forgive him for the
shit he's done."

Which makes me wonder: what heart-wrenching
altercation went down between them that is worth holding a fuming grudge over and leaving one with a crevice
to the very bone? "Okay," I sigh, "how about we talk
about this when you're ready to talk about it." If he ever

will want to talk about his troubles. "Are you okay with that?"

"Yes."

"Okay."

———

For the entire car ride home till the moment we stepped into the house, I've been contemplating whether or not to pop the question: did Cole come to see you?

But I suppose he would've been the happiest man in the world and wouldn't have acted how he did earlier if he did get to see him. He's still the peculiar, frowning Ian.

"Hey, you free to talk?"

"Um," He carefully sets down his wet paintbrush before replying, "as long as it's not about stuff that already happened, yeah, sure."

Arctic... why does he despise the past so much? "It's about someone."

He quickly raises a brow. "No."

"Not him. Cole."

"What about Cole?"

"Did you see him?"

"No. Was I supposed to see him, but he never showed because he doesn't care? It's not surprising."

"Just asking… damn, you didn't have to say he doesn't care." He doesn't know much yet. Thinking about it, neither do I.

"Next."

"I want to know about your whole ordeal with J—"

"No, no, we're not talking about that! What did I just say?"

"I know what you just said." The past is the main source of his current behaviour. And if I want to try to help him—and figure out who to stay away from, since he was right about Shane and his dad—I'm going to have to force myself to plunge deeper into the mine. "But I need to know."

"What for?" He chuckles, "It took a lifetime to get you to listen to me about Shane, and now you're asking about one of your "good friends" who really isn't a friend for you anymore. Go find out for yourself."

I bite my lip. "I want to help you."

Without hesitation to think about it, he flares, "With what? I am fine, I feel fine, there is nothing wrong with me. So, good luck trying to fix something that isn't broken."

I immediately cross my arms, glaring, "Okay, so if you aren't broken, and you feel 'fine' like you love to say, spill why you're so stubborn with talking about your past and why you have problems with people other than mom." Mainly, the people I am friends with.

"That's none of your business."

"No, I'm serious. If you're fine, then you can tell me. Shane bullied you, I understand why you hate him, but you threatened Jayden for no reason, and I'm starting to think you hate these people because they're my friends and you're just paranoid."

"That wasn't for no reason, and I'm not paranoid. I will tell you when you promise me you can keep your lips closed and your ears open and not assume that I'm spewing bullshit. And don't tell anybody else, please. Consider yourself lucky you're someone I trust."

"I promise. Tell me everything."

"Sit down."

———

Back during his sophomore year in the university, he attended while still living in Prince Edward Island, he had a roommate named Itzel—who he had a crush on, and who was Jayden's then-girlfriend. Suddenly, a petty rumour that Ian was having sex with Itzel surfaced about the campus, Jayden got ahold of it and wanted revenge. Ian wasn't and never will be the party type, and everyone knew that. Jayden and Itzel were sorority affiliates, inviting nonaffiliated friends to frat parties wasn't anything to be skeptical about.

Jayden invited Ian to a party without informing Itzel, so she had no idea he was at the same party and couldn't watch out for him. They persuaded Ian to drink and then eventually got him wasted.

He woke up the following morning discovering all of his clothes were missing and his entire body ached. So he was forced to scavenge the room to find every piece of his clothing before sprinting across the campus back for their dorm room naked and with a throbbing hangover because he was late for one of his classes. And luckily Itzel was in there to unlock the door for him.

Discerning that he was sexually assaulted in the midst of his first class, the first person he went to was Itzel.

She told him she was at the same party that night, but she didn't see him, didn't expect him to be there. She left early then called and texted him a few times upon finding he wasn't in their room. He got straight to telling her that her boyfriend invited him to that party, got him drunk, then sexually assaulted him. And that led to Itzel breaking up with Jayden a couple of days later. It pissed him off, and Ian began to receive threatening texts from unknown numbers—most likely Jayden's friends. Instead of leaving the matter in the hands of the police, she took it into her own hands and distanced herself from Jayden and people who were associated with him to support Ian.

Fast forward to a week later, Itzel left Ian in their room to attend a frat party one evening and didn't come back later that night as she said she was. She was pronounced dead at the hospital due to alcohol poisoning the following day.

Not only did it infuriate Ian—he knew Jayden played a huge, if not the leading, role in her death—but it lacerated his world when he was finally able to process the tragedy mentally and emotionally and the fact that she's never coming back; realizing he never got to tell her he loved her.

He witnessed Jayden turn away from her coffin to leave after making eye contact with him before her funeral service. He swore to himself to never forgive him from that day on and got the watercolour dragon inked on himself in honour of her. He's only recently started visiting her grave on her birthday.

Unfortunately, that wasn't the end of Jayden, and Ian continued to see him around the campus; he never got prosecuted or incarcerated due to the lack of evidence, and he had obtained, the money to excuse himself and replenish his reputation.

———

"But she did come back… as you. I see so much of her in you."

"What? I do—" With a fervid passion for fucking with my mind and my emotions, he gazes into my eyes and encloses just above my hips with his arms, his confident lips close in for mine before I could finish my sentence. Conveying electrifying sensations throughout the courses of our bodies, I accede to his move on me. But an ailing vibe that shortly surges over me like a current of water forces me to draw away.

With an expression of utter confusion starting to overcome his face, he quickly asks, "Are you okay?"

I nod, "I'm fine… I'm okay."

"Are you sure?"

"I'm sure."

I don't stop him. Hinting fondness, he willingly proceeds to kiss me, gently guiding his lips along the facet of my neck, and tinkering with the button of my jeans with one of his hands. And as soon as he works his way to unclasp the button, the nails of my left hand immediately delve into the skin of his; expecting him to at least utter a yelp.

"That doesn't hurt me." He whispers. "Relax… I don't want to hurt you again." He seizes my clutch on him, starting at a slow pace with directing his hand into my jeans.

And myself wanting to play off as being a bit chancy, I snag his cock just before he lets out a chuckle from his throat. He asks, "Are you scared or are you just following my actions?"

"Both." Our hands stay motionless for the minute lingering over us as we begin to mentally undress each other with our eyes. I can feel him stiffening in his jeans, aroused and as well cautious of my unpredictability. Should I make the next move? Don't be a wussy, Rae-lynn.

Unsure of my motives for him and leaning in for another make-out session, his hand still in my jeans, proceeds to caress me. I fall a little behind, tanked up on arousal and adrenaline, I gain the courage to undo the button, then unzip his fly. I ain't afraid to say what I see, he has a big dick. And I guess now you're expecting me to go on and on about it for the following ten minutes like in those cheesy romance and erotica novels even I take guilty pleasure in reading. But I'm not. "You want me to…"

Already knowing what I was going to say, he interrupts me with an immediate response. "Hell no! If you put your mouth there, I'm gonna vomit. Use your hand, please."

That's new. I don't know one guy who doesn't like getting blowjobs. I cup my hand firmly around his shaft, starting with long and deliberate strokes, as he goes on with using his daring hand on me, eventually getting it to slip past my panties to further explore my body underneath my clothing to his desire. Then we immediately feel the room surrounding us intensifying as we're both nearing climax.

He gushes first, leaving runnels of warm and sticky semen on my hand. Seconds after, an explosion of sheer alleviation overtakes my body.

"Holy shit," He exhales, "you're good."

"You are too."

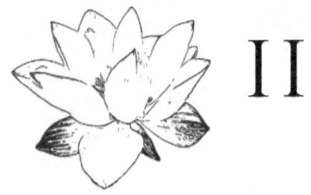 II

NOW IS THE TIME TO purchase a plane ticket to Toronto without Ian being on my ass about it.

My best friend Taura—who graduated with me and lives near her family in Toronto, promised to help me out on my mission.

Just before finally booking my flight, I hear the sound of a gunshot outside, too close for comfort. Keeping in mind that Ian left more than an hour ago and the nearest neighbours live about a mile away, I get up to take a peek from a nearby window. "Who the fuck...?" And then another one pierces the very drums of my ears just as I close the curtains; coming from behind the house. "What the fuck?" I whisper to myself. I maneuver to the hallway, proceeding with creeping to the balcony door, where I look through the glass to find no one in the backyard but hear a third pellet launch from within the woods behind the lake. Then a fourth one, then a fifth one, proceeding to fire within seconds of each other. I fetch my phone to alert the authorities.

But this hidden war doesn't go on for eternity. The final and most ear-shattering pellet—as if it had been shot from a shotgun—is launched the second my brother enters the house. "What was that?!"

"Close the door! It was a gunshot."

"I'm not about to close the door on police officers."

"They're here already? Holy shit." Manifesting before his figure, a lanky woman with dark evening brown eyes and short sun-bleached blonde hair stands with a firm hand on her tactical belt. And before she could make out a word, I unwittingly interrupt, "I called…"

But I end up cluttering my sentence, "there was a…
um, a shootout in the woods behind here…"

Somehow, she can still understand me. "Did you see
someone with a gun?"

"I didn't."

She nods, "We'll let you know if we find anything."

"Thank you." I need to prepare for this damn flight.
I quickly turn my back, contemplating: should I leave
him home tonight for him to wake up clueless of where
I went, or tell him ahead of time I'll be in Toronto for a
day or two? I know he'll be pissed at me when he wakes
up if I don't tell him. "Ian," I turn back around,
"Whoa. You… got a haircut." I've been wondering
what he'd look like without the longer, layered style. "It
looks nice…"

"Thank you, my little flower." Attempting to tease me, he does what a lot of my taller friends have grown used to doing to me… resting his arm atop my head. He adds, "I can tell you have something else on your mind. And it's not about work or this situation."

"Flower?" I snicker, "Is that your way of sweet talking me?"

"No, it's just something I thought you'd like me to call you."

"Hmph." Sarky. "There's nothing else on my mind. At least, not right now." But he knows. Likely by being aware of the frequencies of my neural oscillations going wired as we stare at each other for a fleet minute.

"I hope you aren't lying."

"I do have to tell you something though."

"Mhmm, I know. What's that?"

"I'm going to Toronto tomorrow, just for like a couple of days, and I hope you'll be fine without me." And hope Teddie won't kick my ass if she finds out.

I've been preparing for his anger to flare, but it doesn't, and he shrugs my answer off dismissively. "I'll be fine, I have nine lives, thank you for caring. But what for?"

"I… I'm just going to see my best friend, Taura."

"Taura… sounds familiar."

"Yeah, I have to go pack." I'm really not in the mood to hear another horror story about someone I know.

———

Turns out there was something—someone with a handgun left after that gunfight; found bleeding out from multiple pellet wounds on the shoulder of the sewage ditch that runs to Halifax. Jesus.

I'm not just going to see Taura, I have another thing in mind. According to her and her three younger siblings who see Shane around the campus, he is free to have a private consultation with me.

"Ian." I push open his room door. "I'm leaving." For once he isn't distracted by music or painting; he's lying in bed… naked. I don't think I've ever seen him in bed past 8:30. "What the hell…" I mumble to myself. I should've knocked first.

In a raspy—I just woke up—voice muffled by a pillow, he replies with, "Yeah… okay. Love you."

"I… love you too." And then I entirely forget to tell him not to tell Teddie I left the province if she will be showing up any time soon.

Hauling only a knapsack on my back and my purse on my shoulder, not having to worry about a suitcase and a baggage fee, getting through TSA, and getting to the gate earlier than the crowd was icing on a cupcake. Reminds me of the times I never had to use a suitcase while travelling with my dad when I was a little girl, and even when I was a teenager.

———

"I got banned from going home for two weeks while there was an investigation going on, so I had to stay with our aunt. She showed me the evidence after I came back from talking to his dad, and we find out not only our mom attacked him like she always does, she had Shane's dad with her, and he injected 15 fucking millilitres of liquid heroin into him, almost killed him! And I know that when Kyle is involved in something, Shane almost always is too."

"I'd like to see him try to lie to you and say he isn't."

"If he even says anything to me because I told his mom to send him a message that we were over the same day all of that started. He never answered any of my calls, so I'm sure he got it, and he doesn't care because he acts and thinks like his dad, who is also a fucking clusterfuck like our mom! Oh, they're perfect for each other."

Taura shakes her head. "You sound very tired of everybody's shit."

"I am." There's really no words to accurately describe how fed up I am.

If only we all could somehow go back in time to make ourselves avoid meeting certain people and create an alternate reality. But life presents shitty people to our lives for reasons, and we maintain connections with them until they intentionally (or unintentionally) fuck up.

And now here we are, waiting for one of her siblings to call or text her information on Shane.

Her phone suddenly chimes and she quickly unlocks it to translate a text from one of her brothers in their native language—Spanish to English—aloud to me: 'Tengo una foto de su calendario. Saldrá de la clase en media hora. Puedes venir ahora a esperar los últimos diez minutos.' [I have a picture of his schedule. He will leave the class in half an hour. You can come now to wait for the last ten minutes.]

"You have your ID?"

"Yes."

 I2

MY MIND IS MORPHING ITSELF into a black hole of rage as we wait. Half of it is trying not to beat itself up for not being able to see the horrible reality of him and the other half is already blaming itself for turning a blind eye and not taking the warnings I was given from friends and my own brother seriously. I had to love him, I had to care for him, I had to clear his name, and now I just want to punch myself in the face for wasting valuable time, then maybe mutilate one of his limbs.

"Be nice to him. I'm not letting you get locked up."

"I'll try." I would be mean because I have every right to be, for Ian and myself. "Hey, ponytail!"

The only name that will make him stop in his tracks to look over his shoulder. After taking one more step, he finally does so, then turns around. "What Raelynn?"

Well shit, he answered. "What?" I snicker. "You say that like you don't know why I'm here. Bring your ass over here."

He blinks at me, before taking a baby step backwards "I don't know why you're here. How'd you get in?"

"Don't worry about that. I want answers. Tell me where your dad is."

"I don't know where my dad is, and I don't give a fuck about him."

"Don't lie to me."

"I haven't talked to my dad in a year. If I had an idea of where I wouldn't tell you. Why do you care?"

"You fucking know something. That sack of shit nearly killed my brother, left him to die, and now you expect me to cower in a corner and not say anything? Oh, and he ran off with our mother, what the fuck is that about?"

He rolls his eyes. "I haven't talked to him. I'm sorry. I don't know anything."

"If you won't tell me anything, then I'll ask Megan." He knows his mom loves me. He immediately purses his lips, and I smile. "Hmph. Speak of the devil."

"She wouldn't tell you shit. Dad would beat her ass."

"Really? Now I know that's not true. Otherwise, she wouldn't have tried to warn me about your illegal drug runs with him and your feud with my brother when we started dating. I didn't understand then, but now I do now that I've met him. And now you're my ex-boyfriend."

"Yeah… I don't know who your brother is."

"Ask her whenever."

"I don't…" He sighs in annoyance, "I don't know where my dad is, but I know where your mom is. Last time I heard from him, he was home, your mom is somewhere in Alberta."

How and why would he know that? "What? Are you bullshitting me?"

"You got your answer, now fuck off."

"Then how do you know? You've talked to your dad, didn't you? You're lying to me!" Kyle's the only one who would know exactly where she is. My strategy to trawl clear answers out of him is growing insufficient, and he's beginning to take notice and take advantage of it. "Screw this. You're fucking useless." Forgetting he gets bitter when lousy words are thrown, at him in particular, I throw the word 'useless' at him. He makes me regret it, kind of… by giving me a nice and painful slug in the face that causes me to stagger backwards, almost falling onto my ass.

Now hold on. It's acceptable to make someone like Ian feel like they deserve all the hate in this world, but when it's another human with whatever gives them more benefits, it's suddenly illegal.

I can feel all of the blood rushing to my face. Taura catches one of my arms. "We got to go! You're not about to fight him!"

But I snatch my arm from her grip, wipe the pooling blood from under my nose, then risk a short chase after him until I get close enough to clinch a fistful of his ponytail and tug at it. Bystanders watch in horror as the blood show rouses when I begin to bash his face using the protected side of my phone. Again, and again, and again.

"LET'S GO!" She shouts before hauling me away from the now bloody site.

———

I know I had the choice to walk away. But I was raised solely by my dad, and he taught me to be a functional human and not take shit from anybody.

"Shit… busted my whole damn eye." My left eye is swollen almost shut with a purple, nearly black, hue surrounding it. I apply pressure to it with a small ziplock filled with frozen peas.

"You're going back home with that?" Taura asks.

"I have to. I can't leave my brother alone for too long." And I'm going to have to face him and tell him what happened; he's going to ask a lot of questions. I didn't tell him about the confronting Shane part. "Thank you for helping me… and saving my ass."

"Always."

"Do you still have any hair dye?"

"I do," She squints, "but not any exotic colours."

"How you know I need an exotic colour?"

"In case you need to hide from the Mounties. You know how Shane likes to be a King cobra and twist the truth…"

"That fucker would lie on me."

 13

"OW, SHIT." THE ENTIRE BRUISE is tender to touch, but I have to slather it with a foundation to make it less noticeable. Hopefully, airport security will let me fly back to Halifax nearsighted with only one eye open.

"Whooa," My best friend gazes, "you look like Ariel. Put a seashell top on. Ready?"

"Maybe next Halloween, and I don't have a Prince Eric. But… thank you? Very ready."

"Your brother can be him."

"No, shut up."

———

After an annoying course of people (including TSA) taking notice of my bruised eye and asking what happened, I arrive in Halifax wanting to throat punch the next person that asks. So I keep my head low the entire 15-minute walk from the gate to the parkade. And I finally get home after cautiously driving half-blind—I know it's dangerous—to find large boxes out on the veranda, and the furniture in the lounge moved from their spots and turned over on their backs. "Oh my God!" I groan, not even wanting to know what went on while I was gone.

"Girl, chill out, I'm not dead." I hear my brother's voice from atop the stairs. "You're back just in time."

"What the hell are you doing?" I ask after looking up at him.

Reluctant to answer my question first, he strides down the staircase handling something heavy in his hands, a large box, and when he makes it to the last step, he sets it on the floor in front of him, then gives me a long, fervid glare into my soul. "Before you ask me any question, answer this. And if you lie to me, I will know, so I suggest you tell the truth. What the hell happened to your face and why did you dye your hair?"

"I got punched."

"By who?"

"Shane."

"I'm not surprised!" He snarls. "Thank you for telling me the truth. I know what you did, and now you're hiding because you know you just fucked up."

"And how did I fuck up? He hit me first, and I smashed his fucking face in, he deserved it!"

"It's online for everybody to see now. And now not only am I in trouble, but you just got yourself involved, and now you are too."

Of course, I have no idea who else or what I could be in trouble with because he loves to leave out substantial puzzle pieces for me to figure out for myself. "For what? He should've never put his fucking hands on me."

He raises both of his hands in front of him, "Never mind, I'll explain later." He picks up the box, "Teddie's coming so I can use her truck for all of this shit."

"What is all of that?"

"It's Joselyn's shit because she's staying the fuck out of my house from now on."

Why so suddenly? He should've kicked her out years ago. "Oh... so why did you move all of the...?"

"Why don't you go look in the kitchen and see for yourself. And take that makeup off!"

Set on the island in the kitchen are multiple, maybe more than 15 plastic bags, large and tiny. And the closer I get to the table, the more I am able to recognize the substances inside of them. White and brown powders— almost like grams and kilograms of white and brown sugar, and even rocks that appear like the little crystals and quartz all over the ground outside.

But it's not sugar, and the rocks aren't quartz.

"Is that the semi truck motherload?" I hear Teddie ask from behind, causing me to hurtle myself into one of the chairs in front of me. "Are you okay? No... I know you aren't because you were somewhere you weren't supposed to be, fighting Shane."

I'm already tired of being blamed for his reaction. "You too?" I groan.

"What happened to your eye?"

"THE PRICK PUNCHED ME! He hit me first, so what, you expect me to let him get away with it?!"

"You could've handled it better by telling the campus police. It doesn't matter who hit who first, you don't know him as much as you think you do, he's a dangerous person. And now that you've pissed him off even more and provoked him, he will find a way to get you back."

"What do you know? He knows not to fuck with me."

Maybe I did fuck up like they're saying, but not purposely to stir the pot.

"More than you, Raelynn," She assures, "he and his father are dangerous people, they'll find ways to tear you apart if you don't leave this to Ian."

"And you expect me to let them kill him?"

"No, b—"

"They've been "killing him" for years until he finally decided to clap back. What aren't you telling me?"

Her face turns tense. "Raelynn… leave it alone. I get that you're worried and you want to help Ian. But you don't need to be involved. All you need to do is keep your eyes on him, protect him if you need to, within a safe distance."

"Nice, for once I'll listen to your advice." Another thing I wouldn't understand—as Ian said. Is searching for answers off limits too? I don't want just to sit back and watch everybody eventually get themselves hurt or killed, even if it means I will endure the same fate. To keep the tension at bay, I leave the kitchen, then head upstairs to my room to remove the foundation on my eye.

———

"Raelynn… Rae…" Ian calls my name with a low voice, gently shaking me awake with a hand on my shoulder.

I don't remember falling asleep. I respond with my eyes still closed, "Hmm… what Ian?"

"We need to talk." He says.

"I don't want to talk."

"Raelynn!"

"And let me guess," I reply before sitting up, "give me an hour-long lesson about fucking up? Ian, I don't want to hear it! As long as you are able to keep whatever you… and Teddie apparently, is trying to keep me from finding out, nothing else matters. I'll stay out of it. Please, just fucking pretend I'm not here."

"Actually…" His voice trails off. "I was going to say I don't need you putting your life on the line for me."

"You're welcome."

He presses his lips together firmly, indicating that he's going to blow a fuse if I don't shut my mouth and keep my ears open. "You want me to say thank you for getting yourself hurt for me? Or even worse, you could've gotten killed."

"No." I cross my arms. "I want one since I went all the way out there not to cause a kerfuffle, but to get answers about Kyle and Joselyn's whereabouts, and getting a fucking shiner because you won't TELL ANYBODY SHIT! And, that I even give a fuck about you enough to crave answers! You could've died! I thought we were done with the secret keeping!"

"Rae... I can't..."

"Unless you're going to tell me what you're trying to hide, I don't want to hear anything else. You're giving them more power by staying silent."

"If you would just listen, I'd tell you why I need to stay silent." He lets out a defeated sigh, rather quickly taking in the fact that I probably won't be letting my guard down anytime soon until he gains the courage to spill everything aloud to me. "I get it. I'm sorry." He finally gives up. Almost immediately after he leaves me alone in my room, I exempt the knot in my throat I've been choking back all day.

I'm striving to help him, but he pushes me away on purpose. He's my brother, I'm supposed to care about him as much as I do. I know he can't fight this war alone anymore.

14

THEY MOST LIKELY LEFT THE drugs to set Ian up when they nearly murdered him. Or maybe they needed an unusual spot to hide their package, probably believing they were going to be able to come back and retrieve it. It's gone now. To spare us from having to deal with the authorities for the hundredth time, Teddie decided to bunch all of the bags into a large box and take it with her.

Before she left, I caught her in time to ask her the question I've wanted to know the answer to, since she's the only one who knows I went to go tell Cole about Ian. "Why didn't Cole go see Ian while he was in the hospital?" I whispered.

"I told him not to. Don't worry about why... just stay out of trouble."

"Okay." Trying to stay out of trouble while living with someone like Ian, and Ian himself, is one of the hardest tasks ever for me—and I'm sure for a lot of other people as well. Why? Because he's impulsive.

When I am back inside, and still a bit exhausted from everything, I am rudely berated by him. Clutching my face by my lower jaw, he growls, "I'm not done with you."

"Well, can you not grab my fucking face, please!" I retort before pulling his arm away from my face.

"I know you're not talking to me with that attitude."

"I am. You don't get to do whatever you want to me." I am quick to realize I'm dead wrong, again.

Knowing that I can't really do much when I'm angry because he's twice my size—and pissing him off has become a rational phobia for me—when I turn my back to him, he immediately forces something like a scarf over my mouth. I clench onto the scarf with both of my hands, struggling to yank it from my face.

"You're in my house, sweetheart," He whispers into my ear, "I'm almost obligated to do whatever I want to you." After successfully knotting the ends behind my head, he drags me back towards the couch. Not again. "But since you want to be a smart ass…"

He sets me face down onto the couch, proceeding with attempting to strip me by tugging at the waistband of my jeans as I squirm underneath him. But he suddenly stops himself before he could cause further damage, and just stares at me, motionless as I begin to sob hysterically. "I… I'm… sorry, I…" He stammers, quickly loosening his grip around my wrists. And after thinking to himself for at least a minute or two, he finally lowers the scarf from over my mouth.

"Sorry?! You're sorry?" I snap through tears. Now I know he really didn't mean his apology for the last time. In infuriation and distress, I numbly gain the courage to do what I've wanted to do for a while. I slap him. "Get the fuck away from me!"

He begins to have a full-blown nervous breakdown, hyperventilating, shaking, and crying right in front of me. And just when the blood flowing through my veins simmers quick enough to make me scream, "WHAT THE FUCK IS WRONG WITH YOU?!" at him, he collapses onto his knees, repeatedly apologizing to the point he could no longer make out the words, "I'M SORRY!" or even a complete sentence.

The overwhelming tension forces me to storm out of the lounge, abandoning him in the midst of his breakdown.

 15

I SHOULD'VE LEFT WHEN I had the chance. Now I'm stuck having to look after my brother when all I want to do is stay a thousand or more kilometres away from him. Unfortunately, I can't just get up and leave him. Not until Teddie announces it's safe to do so.

There's no excuse for what he has done to me, and he knows that. A simple apology isn't going to heal anything. It's not my job to be his personal punching bag.

My only choice now is to scorn him until he finally gets the memo that I am no longer putting up with his shit and would instead be left alone. It's been almost a week since I've begun my silent treatment for him, just giving him a blank stare whenever he tries to strike up a conversation and refusing to acknowledge his existence.

"Raelynn…" Ian utters a moan, proceeding with rubbing up against me like an attention craving puppy, "please talk to me."

Refusing to answer or succumb to his plea for attention by keeping myself occupied with one of my books, I scoot myself to the other end of the couch; farther away from him.

"What are you reading?" He asks, attempting to distract me from noticing he's moving closer. I keep my mouth shut. He stops scooting closer to think to himself for a split-second—possibly another excuse to make me feel bad for him. "I am so sorry for hurting you, Raelynn. I know you think I don't mean it. I got carried away, and I went ballistic on you…" He suddenly trails off, probably to see if I'm paying attention. I keep my head down, but he proceeds to talk, "Because I got triggered. But I know it's not an excuse to hurt you. There is no excuse for hurting you." He pauses again. "I have

a lot of things to tell you. The secrets I've been… keeping from you. I was afraid to tell you because she
would've killed me for telling you."

I slightly raise my head, to immediately indicate to
him that I'm listening.

"I'm a sex slave. Those scratches on my back, and
what you saw before Joselyn knocked you unconscious
that night, she raped me. It's nothing new to me. I've
been sold to various people, women in particular, in ex-
change for money and drugs as young as four years
old… four times a month, I was forced to be a random,
abusive person's slave."

Oh my God.

"I never told my dad anything, I thought he knew at
first, then I found out he didn't know when she threatened to kill him and sell me if I told him or anybody. I

love my dad, he was my only light, and I fucking miss him. I feel so fucking stupid and selfish for not telling him anything when all he did was worry and put me first before himself."

I part my lips, but I'm at a loss for words. I close my book before turning my head to face him, my eyes meeting his now tear-filled eyes.

"You saved my life," He sniffs, "when I met you, you gave me the feeling my dad and Itzel gave me… like I could tell you anything… like you wouldn't hurt me. You're the last person I would want to walk away or die. But now that I'm still staying silent about her, there are other people, and children, under her control." The tears rimming his eyes begin to descend desperately down his cheeks. "I'm so sorry, Raelynn. I felt dead after hurting you, I still feel dead. Crying and hurting myself wasn't enough, nothing can amount to the pain of seeing you in pain, and I know nothing is going to completely repair the traumas and wounds I've inflicted on you."

Offering comfort, without saying a damn word because I really need to shut the fuck up and listen to him, I extend my arms out to him. "I… I'm s-sorry, Ian," I whisper to him as soon as he accepts my comfort offering to sob into my shoulder. "I accept your apology. I'm sorry for ignoring you."

"I love you."

"I… I love you too."

———

According to Ian, Kyle went in on the entire thing in the first place, knew Joselyn was selling Ian to pedophiles and that the mini clusterfuck (Shane) was bullying him. They wanted to kill him because he's too much of a witness of everything they've been doing. And one of the many victims of the trafficking.

Shane wasn't lying about Joselyn being in Alberta. She primarily lives somewhere there, and that's where she runs her "business." She's a kingpin, and Kyle is undoubtedly her main apprentice if there aren't any more people who are loyal to her like he is.

———

"I have a secret to tell you too. I couldn't tell you sooner because both Megan and Teddie told me not to tell you. I know where Cole is."

"How?"

"Megan told me. While you were in the hospital, I went back to Charlottetown to tell him that you were in a coma because of that overdose and he was supposed to go see you, but Teddie told him not to. She didn't tell me why when I asked."

"That bitch."

"I'm sure it must be for a good reason. Teddie wouldn't purposely keep a secret for any of the reasons her sister does. Don't take anything wrong, Cole really loves you, and he misses you. I ended up listening to him and Joselyn arguing about you downstairs that morning you were gone to get the ibuprofen for that headache I had."

The guy nods slowly as his brain is able to process the new information while a gentle and relaxed smile forms on his lips.

"Are you okay now that all of that stress is off of your shoulders?" I ask.

"I feel like a bird."

"Why a bird?"

"Because birds are free. Most of them are."

"Hm. That's true. Oh, and one more thing."

"Yes?"

"Promise," I take both of his hands into mine, "please, no more secret keeping."

"Promise."

 16

"RAE?"

"Hmm?" I groan before turning over onto another pillow. I'm going to take a wild guess that it's not quite 8 yet, but it's a little bit past 7 since Ian is an early bird, usually up and out of bed before 8. "What Ian?"

"Did you leave the balcony door open last night?"

"The wha... no."

He replies with, "Hm... okay." in a slightly concerned, but mostly confused tone before leaving the room. Weird question to ask, considering I have my own door to the balcony and I don't have to use the other one. I close my eyes.

———

And in my dream, I open my eyes again, tracing the outline of the inner hollow in the tray ceiling above me with my eyes calmly for I would say an infinite amount of time. But the fervour doesn't stay long, and I begin to feel a strange weigh-in transpiring. First over my arms and legs, then constricting my neck, forcing me to strive for air. I can't cry, or scream, or move. I can only help-lessly bear the dark force closing in on my throat.

I'm still staring up above me, where the livid silhou-ette of someone familiar begins to manifest in front of me. Ian. Possessing a leaden grey tint to his skin and a maze of discoloured capillaries unfurling and bulging from the thin layer of skin on his face, he gradually worsens the force constricting my neck with one of his hands—also swelling with discoloured capillaries, followed by emitting the most inhuman shriek into one of my ears.

———

"RAELYNN!" I hear my brother call out my name in real life, which causes me to lurch forward out of my dream state… or more like nightmarish state. Wait, I'm still alive? "WHAT?!"

"Come downstairs. Teddie needs you."

Still, a tad bit dazed by the demonic dream I just had about him, I reply, "For what?"

He shifts himself back against the door frame before rolling his eyes at me. "Girl…"

I don't even want to go back to sleep anyway. "Okay," I get out of bed, "I'm up." She's usually already at work at this time. It must be important if she decided to skip work to talk to me.

Finding the box of the drugs she took with her the last time she was here set on the table in front of her, I start to question myself whether it was a smart move of her to take it. "Yes?"

She looks even more beat than usual without her makeup on. Must've been rushing. But she still has her uniform on… late shift? She turns her head towards me, an earnest expression immediately crosses her face upon seeing me. "You didn't let the word out, did you?"

"What word?"

"This." She replies, shooting a quick glance at the box. "Uh, your friend tried to attack me last night, and I had to detain his ass for an hour or so. Somebody told him I had it, and I wonder if it was you."

"Friend? I never told anybody about that."

"His name is Jayden."

Oh, that bitch. "He's not a friend, never will be. I never told him shit."

"Then how…?"

"He's friends with Shane and Shane is involved with his dad and Joselyn, apparently, since he knew and told me she's somewhere in Alberta. He either got it from Shane, or one of those two." But then, somebody had to be around to see her take it.

"I was wrong to take this. I have to go to work soon, we need to bury this now."

"Where?"

"Behind the lake."

"I don't know if that's a good idea," I bite my lip, "there was a gunfight nearby for some reason last week, somebody got injured, and the police officer who came never told us the reason, so I'm still trying to figure out whether that was something for drugs or..." Because nobody goes to a random, secluded place armed and just starts shooting whoever they see there.

She drops her head. "It was." She discloses. "I'm sure you both know Zach, you probably saw him that day you went to go talk to Cole."

"The man with the gold eyes and blond hair, yes I saw him."

"That might've been his wife you were talking to because she's an officer and she knows not to blow his cover. And of course, that fucker Kyle was stupid and crazy enough to shoot him for that package he took from back there."

I shake my head. Kyle being one of the culprits of most of the crazy shit that has been happening lately no longer surprises me. "Nothing special." I don't know why Megan married him.

"Got them." Ian enters the room holding onto a couple of shovels in one arm and one in his other.

———

While ladling out the frozen soil near the littoral of the lake, from the corner of one of my eyes, I catch a glimpse of something gleaming from behind a tree in the vicinity of us.

The small, but steep pit reminds me of the pit I found mom's corpse in during that first strange dream involving Ian I had.

"Don't say a damn word about this." Teddie ensures. "That includes you, Raelynn. None of your friends need to know."

My mouth is not that big. "Never told anybody in the first place." That gleaming light is bothering me. I release my grip on the handle of my shovel, letting it fall to the ground.

"What are you doing?"

"Hold on." I pace towards the tree. The light isn't even moving, it's stilly reflecting the sunlight; it can't be an animal. When I get up and close to it, I reach my arm out to touch it.

"I WOULDN'T TOUCH THAT! LOOK AROUND IT!"

Thanks, Teddie. And so instead of touching the mysterious object, I walk around the tree, only to regret being curious about it in the first place. "Uhh… Teddie!"

"WHAT IS IT?"

"COME LOOK!" The object reflecting in the sun is the silver bracelet of a dead body, dangling by the neck from a rope tied to one of the branches above. "Look who finally decided to make the right choice." It's not just any lifeless body, it's Kyle's lifeless body.

I know it's a horrible thought to even think or say, but he deserves it. I don't feel bad.

"Damn."

"Why on my property?"

"Ian!"

"What? You expect me to pray for him, after all the shit he's done? It doesn't work like that, darling."

17

"I WONDER HOW SHE'S GOING to take this," Ian whispers.

"I don't know. If Teddie wants us to do this, then... I just don't know. Doesn't she think it's a bit harsh to just flat out tell someone's wife their husband committed suicide?"

He purses his lips tensely. "Unless she has a death wish and she's trying to get us killed..."

"I doubt that." Oh boy. Noticing that I am hesitant to knock on the door or ring the doorbell, my brother— being impatient with me—rings the doorbell for me before I could come up with the proper words, or at least an explanation for what Megan is about to hear. "Screw you…" I snarl quietly at him.

"Later."

When she finally answers the door, my mind proceeds to fumble coming up with the first sentence. "H-Hi… Megan," I stammer, "uhh we… have something to, um, tell you." I eventually make out.

"Hello." She smiles.

Growing agitated with my hesitation and anxiousness, Ian sighs, "Jesus Christ… we found Kyle's body in our backyard this morning, hanging from a tree, sadly, and our aunt Teddie sent us to inform you that… yeah, he committed suicide, and he's going straight to hell. Oops…"

"Fucking asshole!" Expecting her to follow up with a bereaved reaction, I mentally prepare myself for a possible breakdown. But she just stares blankly into our eyes.

"Finally," She shrugs, then immediately slides her wedding ring off of her finger, "thank God, tired of being a slave. Thank you for the pleasant information. I've been expecting you two, come in, I have a lot to tell you."

ACKNOWLEDGEMENTS

In loving memory of Christina, Emily, and Charlie.

Thank you, Landon and Kantessa, for staying by my side and believing in me. I love you.